THE MINI TREASURE CHEST OF GREAT FAIRY TALES

D1275631

III
CONTENTS

© DAMI EDITORE, ITALY

Published in 1991 by TORMONT PUBLICATIONS INC.
338 St. Antoine St. East
Montreal, Quebec, Canada H2Y 1A3
Tel. (514) 954-1441   Fax (514) 954-1443

ISBN 2-89429-010-1

Graphic Design and Layout : Zapp
Illustrations : Tony Wolf
              Piero Cattaneo
              Severino Baraldi
Text : Peter Holeinone
Adaptation : Jane Brierley

PRINTED IN CANADA

TORMONT

HANSEL AND GRETEL

Once upon a time, a poor woodcutter lived in a tiny cottage in the forest with his two children, Hansel and Gretel. Their mother had died, and the woodcutter's second wife often ill-treated the children. She was forever nagging the woodcutter.

"There isn't enough food for us all. We must get rid of the two brats!" declared the stepmother. She kept pestering her husband to abandon his children in the forest.

"Take them miles from home, so they'll never find their way back. Maybe someone else will take them in." The unhappy woodcutter didn't know what to do.

Hansel comforted his sister. "Don't worry, Gretel. If they leave us in the forest, we'll find the way home." He slipped out of the house and filled his pockets with little white pebbles, then went back to bed.

All night long the woodcutter's wife nagged at her husband. At last, as the sun was rising, he led Hansel and Gretel into the forest.

Hansel secretly dropped the little white pebbles on the mossy green ground. All too soon, however, the woodcutter plucked up the courage to desert them. He mumbled an excuse and was gone.

Night fell. Gretel began to sob bitterly. Hansel felt scared, but tried to hide his feelings.

3

"Be brave and trust me! I'll take you home, even if Father doesn't come back!" Luckily the moon was full that night. Hansel waited until its cold light filtered through the trees.

"Now give me your hand!" he said to Gretel. "We'll get home safely, you'll see!" The tiny white pebbles gleamed in the moonlight, and the children found their way home. They crept in through a half-opened window without waking their parents, and slipped into bed.

Next day, when their stepmother discovered that Hansel and Gretel had returned, she flew into a rage. "Why didn't you do as I told you!" she shrieked at her husband.

The weak woodcutter was torn between shame and the fear of disobeying his cruel wife, who kept Hansel and Gretel under lock and key all day. They had nothing to eat but a crust of bread.

All night, the husband and wife quarreled, but when dawn came the woodcutter once again led the children into the forest.

Hansel, however, had not eaten his bread. As he walked through the trees, he left a trail of crumbs behind. But the little boy had forgotten about the hungry birds. They flew along the trail, and in no time had eaten all the crumbs.

Again, the woodcutter left the children with a lame excuse.

"I've made a trail, like last time!" Hansel whispered to Gretel. Alas, when night fell, they saw to their horror that all the crumbs had gone.

"I'm frightened!" wept Gretel bitterly. "I'm cold and hungry and I want to go home."

"Don't be afraid. I'm here to look after you!" said Hansel, but he shivered at the deep shadows and glinting eyes in the darkness.

All night the two children huddled together for warmth at the foot of a large tree. When dawn broke, they wandered about the forest looking for a path. Hope soon faded. They were well and truly lost. On and on they walked, until suddenly they came upon a curious cottage in the middle of a glade.

They drew closer to the little house.

"Why, this is chocolate!" gasped Hansel as he broke a lump of plaster from the wall.

"And this is icing!" exclaimed Gretel, putting another piece of wall in her mouth. Starving but delighted, the children began to eat pieces of candy broken off the cottage.

"Isn't this delicious?" said Gretel with her mouth full.

"We'll stay here," Hansel declared.

They were just about to try a piece of the biscuit door when it swung quietly open. An old woman with a crafty gleam in her eye peered out.

"Well, well! Aren't you the sweet-toothed little darlings! Come in, come in! You've nothing to fear," cackled the crone, opening the door wide.

No sooner were they inside than the witch — for it was indeed a witch — grabbed Hansel and squeezed his arm. "You're nothing but skin and bones. I'll have to fatten you up!" she snorted, locking him in a cage.

"You can do the housework," she told Gretel grimly, "then I'll make a meal of you too!"

As luck would have it, the witch had very weak eyes. "Let me feel your finger!" she would say to Hansel every day, to check if he were any fatter. But Gretel had given him a chicken bone and smeared the witch's spectacles with butter. When the old woman went to touch his finger, he held out the bone instead.

"Much too thin!" she would complain.

One day the witch grew tired of waiting. "Light the oven," she told Gretel. "We're going to have a tasty boy for dinner!" A little later the impatient old crone snapped, "Run and see if the oven is hot yet!"

Gretel returned, whimpering, "I can't tell if it's hot enough."

"Nitwit!" the witch screamed. "I'll see for myself." She bent down to peer inside the oven. Gretel gave her a tremendous push and slammed the door shut!

There was a screech and a sizzle, and that was the end of the witch. Gretel ran to free her brother. Just to be on the safe side, they fastened the oven door with a large padlock.

The children feasted on the candy house until they discovered a huge chocolate egg. They broke off a piece. There inside lay a casket of gold coins!

"We'll take the treasure with us," said Hansel. The two children filled a large basket with food and set off through the forest in search of their home. Luck was with them, and on the second day they saw their father coming toward them, weeping.

"Thank God I have found you," he cried. "Your stepmother is dead. Come home with me now, my dear children!"

Hansel and Gretel hugged their father with all their might. "Promise you'll never desert us again," said Gretel.

"Look, Father," said Hansel, opening the casket. "We're rich now. You'll never have to chop wood again!"

And so they all lived happily together ever after.

THE SEVEN CROWS

Once upon a time, far away amid high mountains, there was a green valley with a clear stream running through it. Here a woodsman had built his house. He lived there with his wife, seven sons, and one daughter.

The woodsman was often away, and his wife had a hard time bringing up the children alone. The daughter was kind, pretty, and helpful. But the boys were a terrible problem —rude, disobedient, and quarrelsome. They had no respect for their mother, and she was at her wits' end.

The poor woman kept her sorrow to herself instead of telling her husband, not realizing that it only made things worse. The boys' sister suffered most. She loved her brothers, despite their detestable behavior, but most of all she loved her mother.

One day the seven boys did the wickedest thing yet. In the woods grew a dangerous grass that made animals' stomachs swell. The woodsman had always warned his sons never to let the goats eat it.

The cruel boys filled a bag with the grass and mixed it with the animals' fodder. Soon, the goats and even the cow fell ill. Their stomachs swelled and they couldn't stand up.

"What will we do for milk? We won't be able to make any cheese!" cried the mother. "How will we survive?" The mischievous sons laughed, not realizing the evil they had done.

"I wish you were crows rather than sons of mine!" sobbed the woman in desperation. As she spoke these words, a black cloud overshadowed the sun, and the boys turned into seven big crows. They flew away, croaking miserably.

The woman was filled with fear and remorse. When the father came back from work the next day, he was shocked and saddened by the news of his sons' behavior and their terrible fate. He tried to comfort his wife, telling her it wasn't her fault. All the same, the house was filled with gloom.

A long time passed and the little girl grew older. She still remembered her brothers and rarely smiled. One day she asked her mother's permission to go and look for them.

"I'll find them, I know it. Please let me go!"

The mother couldn't resist her daughter's pleas, and the little girl left home with a small bundle of provisions. For two days she walked through the woods, climbing toward the mountains. Soon she had no more food. Her clothes were torn and she was cold and tired.

At dawn on the third day, she came upon a strange cottage in the mist.

Something drew her to the house, despite its uninviting appearance. Inside, she found a low table with seven bowls on it, and her heart beat very fast. Maybe she had found what she was looking for!

There was a large pot full of oatmeal on the fire. The little girl was very hungry, so she poured some of the oatmeal into a bowl and gulped it down. Then she went upstairs. There she found seven tiny beds. Tears rose to her eyes as she realized her search was at an end. Exhausted by the journey, she lay down on one of the beds and fell asleep.

Some time later, seven chattering crows pushed open the front door and sat down at the table.

"Someone's been eating our oatmeal," said one of the crows, inspecting the dirty bowl.

"But who would ever come up here?" said another.

When the crows had finished eating, they pulled on their sleeping caps and went upstairs. How surprised they were to find a little girl in one of the beds!

One of the crows pecked delicately at a braid. "But this is — "

"Our sister!" they all cried. At that moment the little girl opened her eyes. The sight of the crows scared her at first. But then she jumped up and held out her arms.

"I've found you! I've found you!" she cried joyfully.

"Will you come home with me?" she asked.

"We'd love to go back," replied the seven crows sadly, "and we're sorry for our evil ways. But how can we show ourselves to our parents like this?"

"Mother keeps crying and thinking of you," the little girl insisted, and soon she had convinced her brothers to make the journey.

"There's no need to walk over the mountains," said the brothers. "We'll fly there and carry you."

As they were about to leave, the youngest brother called, "Wait a minute! Let's bring Mother all the sparkling stones we've found."

"They might be precious, you know," added another brother. "When we crows see something sparkle, we can't help snapping it up."

"How beautiful!" said the little girl when the crows showed her their bag of treasure. She tucked it carefully in her pocket.

The crows took hold of her tightly, and they all rose up in the air. What a different place the world looked from above! At first the little girl felt very nervous, but her brothers held her firmly. By and by they flew over the valley, the stream, and the little house where they were born. The farmyard was deserted when they landed.

"You wait here and I'll go and call mother," said the little girl. She slipped silently into the kitchen. Her mother sat by the table, weeping.

"I'm back and I have a big surprise!" cried the little girl, hugging her mother.

The poor woman was so happy that she didn't know whether to laugh or cry. When she saw the crows in the farmyard she recognized them at once.

"My poor sons! I missed you so much. Oh, why did I ever utter that curse?"

"We regret all our wickedness too," clamored the crows. Suddenly their voices changed, and instead of seven crows, there stood seven boys.

The father, who had heard voices, came running from the house. "My children!" he cried, embracing his seven lost sons and his daughter.

The sparkling stones turned out to be precious after all, and from that day forward, the family prospered.